Xander and the Rainbow-Barfing Unicorns is published by
Stone Arch Books
a Capstone imprint
1710 Roe Crest Drive
North Mankato, Minnesota 56003
www.mycapstone.com

Cataloging-in-Publication Data is available on the Library
of Congress website.
ISBN 978-1-4965-5715-5 (library binding)
ISBN 978-1-4965-5719-3 (paperback)
ISBN 978-1-4965-5731-5 (eBook PDF)

Summary: Xander Stone is a typical twelve-year-old boy
until he meets the Rainbow-Barfing Unicorns—stinky,
zombielike, upchucking creatures from the magical world
of Pegasia.

Designer: Bob Lentz
Production Specialist: Kris Wilfahrt

Printed and bound in Canada. PA020

by Matthew K. Manning

illustrated by Joey Ellis

MAGIC
SMELLS
AWFUL

STONE ARCH BOOKS
a capstone imprint

LEGEND SAYS . . .

The Rainbow-Barfing Unicorns
come from a faraway, magical
world called Pegasia. Not so long
ago, these stinky, zombielike,
upchucking creatures were
banished to Earth for being,
well . . . stinky, zombielike,
upchucking creatures. However,
Earth presents them with a new
danger: humans.

So, just who are the Rainbow-Barfing
Unicorns . . . ?

CRADIE

(CRAY-DEE)

BLEP

(BLEHP)

RONK

(RAWNK)

CHAPTER ONE

Xander rolled over in bed and looked at his digital clock: 6:29. In one minute, his alarm would go off. In one minute, he could start searching for magic again.

Twenty seconds later, Xander decided waiting for the clock to catch up to him wasn't worth it. He sat up and switched off the alarm before it could do its job.

Then he quickly dropped to the floor and looked under the bed.

Every magic hunter knows that the first place to check for mystical creatures is under the bed. All sorts of things could be lurking there: elves, trolls, or maybe even a gremlin or three.

Little magic things love the shadows that only the bottom side of a mattress can provide. And more than that, they love the secret treasures that often fall between the crack of a bed and the wall.

Xander knew this more than most. He had been a magic hunter for practically all twelve years of his life.

The side of Xander's head rested on the soft white carpet. He peered under the bottom bunk. A year ago, Xander's older sister had shared his room and used the top bunk. Now that she was in her own room, the whole thing belonged to Xander.

The top bunk held nothing but a few science-fiction novels, a reading lamp, and a stack of old comic books. But there would be no magic up there. Not that high. No, the goblins and fairies much preferred places people rarely traveled.

They preferred the *dark* places.

Xander examined the eight inches of space between the mattress and the floor. Nothing was there except for the same dust bunny as yesterday and the same pink rubber ball that rested against the wall's baseboard—just out of Xander's reach. But Xander wasn't fazed. He had plenty of other spots left to check.

The next logical hiding place was the bedroom closet. Like other dark, fairly unused areas, closets were the perfect place to catch a sleeping beastly creature.

Xander tiptoed up to it. The last thing he wanted to do was scare away any monsters or witches before he got a chance to catch them in the act of monstering or witching.

Xander flung open his closet door. "Aha!" he exclaimed.

But the only things he surprised were a rack full of clean clothes and a bin of underwear and socks. To their credit, neither seemed particularly startled.

"Hey, buddy," said a familiar voice from behind Xander. "You up already?"

It was a strange question to ask. Xander was obviously up already. He thought about telling his dad as much.

"Hey, Dad," he said instead. It was much too early for sarcasm.

"Pick out your clothes, and I'll meet you downstairs," said the stocky man standing in the doorway. His dad yawned and removed the thick black glasses from his face. Then he used the end of an oversized T-shirt to clean away any smudges that might have appeared during the night.

Xander had his own theory about the smudges. The work of dust demons, he thought. But he kept that to himself, too.

"You want waffles again?" his dad asked.

"OK," said Xander. He turned around and studied the inside of his closet again.

There wasn't a single sign of a disturbance. Apparently, the closet had been monster-free all night.

The next stop on Xander's list was the wardrobe in the hallway. Xander had it on good authority that these wooden cupboards were quite capable of housing portals to other dimensions. This kind of magical doorway required a different approach.

When Xander cracked the large wooden door open, he did so slowly. These types of portals were often only usable by children. If he had swung the door open too quickly, it would seem as if a grown man was doing it. If that was the case, the portal would seal up in a flash. Magical portals needed to keep their secrets safe from adults. Xander was certain about that.

Inside the wardrobe hung the family's winter coats. Xander took a deep breath and then pushed them aside. He reached to the back of the wardrobe, stretching his arm as far as it would go. His fingers touched the familiar wooden back of the large piece of furniture.

No portal.

No doorway to another world.

He felt around a bit more just to be sure.

"Buddy, waffles are getting cold!" said his father's voice from downstairs.

Xander straightened up. He hadn't even gotten dressed yet.

Five more minutes passed.

If there wasn't any magic to find around his house, Xander would make his own. Now fully dressed, he walked down the stairs. The carpeted stairway creaked its usual creak as he made his way to the kitchen. When he turned the corner, his dad didn't notice him right away.

"You better hurry, guy," said his dad. "It's almost time for school to start, and you've still got your seven-block walk to—"

Xander's dad stood in the kitchen and looked at his son. Where he was expecting to see a fairly short, round-faced, brown-haired sixth grader, stood a *wizard*.

The wizard wore a long gray beard,
a navy cloak that fell to his feet, and a
pointed hat decorated with glow-in-the-dark
stars.

"Huh," said Xander's dad. "This is new."

Xander smiled. Then he sat down at the
table to eat his waffles.

CHAPTER TWO

"Aren't you too old for costumes?"
Xander's dad asked during breakfast.

Xander didn't like defending himself.
He was the quiet type. He usually just
took whatever life threw at him without
complaining.

But today, Xander felt like he needed to
explain things to his dad. "It's 'Dress Like a
Historical Figure Day' at school," he said. "If
I don't wear a costume, I'll get a bad grade."

His dad didn't respond. But Xander was pretty sure he caught him rolling his eyes.

* * *

Things got worse when Xander arrived at school.

"Merlin is *not* a historical figure," his teacher said.

Xander didn't argue. He didn't want to have to talk in front of the entire class. Arguing with his dad was one thing. But arguing with the teacher in public was quite another. If Xander could go the rest of his life without speaking to a crowd, he'd be happy. He got nervous just thinking about it.

Instead, Xander just sat in his chair without saying a word. If he *had* spoken, he would have said, "Merlin is based on Myrddin Wyllt, a famous real-life prophet."

But he didn't say that.

Instead, Xander quietly sat at his desk with his nervous palms sweating and the rest of the class staring at him.

Things weren't better at recess.

"You think it's Halloween?" said his classmate Andy, punching Xander's arm.

Xander kept quiet. He didn't want to make a scene. By then, nearly the entire class had gathered around them.

When Andy started calling him "Halloweenie," the nickname caught on. And it continued for the rest of the day.

By the time school was out, Xander was more than ready to go home. He had no idea that things were about to get even worse.

When the class lined up near the door, Xander saw his friend Kelly laughing along with the rest of the kids.

Kelly had looked as pretty as ever on that day. Xander could see her near the end of the line, standing next to Andy. Kelly, with her sparkling brown eyes, straight brown hair, and her black, trim beard that covered the length of her chin.

She didn't always have a beard. But today she was dressed like Abraham Lincoln. Xander still thought she looked cute despite the facial hair.

He had known Kelly since kindergarten. When they were little, she had joined him on his magic hunts. He remembered countless afternoons where they hiked through the park in their suburb. They hunted for trolls under the tiny bridges that arched over the park's small streams.

As they got older, Kelly joined him less and less. But she never stopped asking about Xander's adventures. Kelly had kept talking to him all these years, even though everyone else thought he was too old for magic.

But when he had looked at Kelly today, he saw the smile on her face.

Everyone was giggling, and Andy was pointing at Xander. Xander turned away. His face grew angry under his itchy, fake beard.

The class filed off into two sections: bus riders and walkers. Xander lived close enough to school that he didn't have to bother with the school bus. But today, he wasn't quite a walker either.

Xander was a runner.

As soon as he got the OK from his teacher, Xander took off down the street as fast as he could go. He ripped off his beard and cap. He threw his navy cloak on the sidewalk as he ran.

Xander didn't check under the bush in Mr. Reed's yard for a gnome hole. He didn't bother to explore the cemetery for any lingering spirits.

He just ran.

Xander wanted nothing to do with magic. The other kids were right. It had just taken him too long to accept it. Magic was as fake as his ridiculous costume. It was as fake as Kelly. It was all nonsense. And Xander was too old for nonsense.

Then, right at that exact moment, Xander saw the rainbow.

CHAPTER THREE

If Xander hadn't been in such a hurry, he would have seen the rainbow earlier. After all, his neighborhood was small, made up of only twenty to thirty houses in a quiet, mountainside valley.

Xander ran faster. As he turned onto his street, two more rainbows shot across the sky from the same starting point. All three were coming from the forest directly behind Xander's house!

When he got to his driveway, Xander needed a moment to catch his breath. He stopped and bent over. He rested his hands on his knees.

Xander had never been the athletic type. He was a little overweight for his age. It was nothing the doctor was worried about. Xander ate really well, in fact. He wasn't big on sweets. Fruits and vegetables had always been his thing, ever since an early age. His family was sure he would grow into his body. His mom and dad said that all the time, even if Xander wasn't sure what it meant.

Either way, Xander was certainly out of breath when he got home. All the lettuce in the world didn't seem to help with that.

While he was panting and also trying

not to pant, Xander looked up at his house. There were the three rainbows. They were already fading into nothingness. Xander's mouth fell further open. It was beautiful.

Had these rainbows happened yesterday, or that morning even, he would have already been running up the mountain, dodging the trees of its thick forest. Rainbows never appeared near his home. Before this afternoon, he wouldn't have missed the chance to hunt for a leprechaun's pot of gold.

But Xander was different now. Or that's at least what he told himself.

By this point, his breath had been successfully caught. Xander was ready to head inside and have an after-school snack. He might even binge watch a TV show or three. He would try anything to take his mind off of school. To take his mind off of Kelly.

He was too old for nonsense, after all.

Xander shook his head. He walked a few more steps toward his front door. Then he stopped—

And ran full speed toward the woods behind his house!

No, this was a sign that Xander couldn't ignore. This was something important.

As he ran, three more completely new rainbows shot across the sky. They didn't simply fade into view, as rainbows are known to do. No, they burst through the air, as if they were in a hurry to get to the other side of the mountain.

This required Xander's attention.

CHAPTER FOUR

Xander ran halfway up the mountain before the rainbows faded again. He knew the trail well. His dad and mom were big hikers. They had taken him up this small mountain almost as soon as he had learned how to walk.

Xander loved the woods, even though he wasn't sure who the land belonged to. Whoever it was, he or she didn't seem to mind the well-worn path cutting up the mountainside.

The only person who really disliked that trail was Xander's sister, Reagan. But she hated most things. His mom said it was a phase she was going through. It had been a very long phase.

By the time Xander had rushed up to the clearing near the top of the mountain, he was no longer sure where the rainbows had been coming from. He assumed it was the mountain's peak. That was just his best guess.

But as he looked around, he saw no trace of gold. There were no leprechauns. He was too late. Plus, he was panting again.

Xander took a minute and caught his breath. What had he been thinking?

He was supposed to be over this magic stuff. What could have possibly been up on this mountain worth all this effort? What could possibly—?

"RONK."

Xander froze in place. Whatever that was, the sound was something Xander had never heard before. He didn't breathe. He didn't move. He just listened.

"Shh!"

Someone was on the mountain with him.

"ROOONK," said a voice from the woods to his left. The sound was longer than last time. The sound was drawn out, but it was quieter.

"He's going to hear you!" whispered a second voice.

"Hello?" Xander said. He was getting a

little freaked out now. Whoever was there was hiding from him. That couldn't be a good thing.

"RONK!" a voice said from the woods.

It sounded happy now. The voice sounded glad to meet him.

"What is the matter with you?" said the second voice. It was a girl. Xander was sure of it. The second person was definitely a girl. Maybe she was his age.

"Kelly?" Xander said, almost under his breath. He wasn't sure why he said it. But he said it just the same.

"RONK!" said the first voice again. It was louder and more excited now.

Xander didn't have time to think about the kind of person who would yell such a weird word. If he thought about it, he would probably realize that it wasn't a word at all. But Xander had no time to think. Because at that very second, an impossible creature was running directly at him.

Xander turned to run away, but he didn't get more than two steps. He fell on his back as the creature pounced on top of him.

Xander looked up at the beast. It was green and looked almost like a pony.

But its skin was gooey and sticky. It was covered in spots of mud and dirt. One of its glowing yellow eyes was lower than the other. And it only had one ear.

Xander had never seen a pony look like this, that was for sure. And then there was the matter of the chipped and crooked horn on the creature's forehead.

"RONK!" the beast brayed again. It almost looked like it was smiling.

Xander closed his eyes. This was it. He was going to be eaten by what just had to be a zombie unicorn. He had finally found magic, and it was going to gobble him up.

"OK, OK," said the strange girl's voice. "I think you're scaring him, Ronk."

The unicorn standing on top of Xander looked at his prey, and then looked away for a second. Then he looked back at Xander.

"RONK?" he said. It sounded almost like an apology.

The unicorn stepped off of Xander and onto the grass of the clearing. Then he looked at the weeds near his hooves. It was like he had never noticed them before. He began chewing at the wild plants.

"Sorry about Ronk," said the girl's voice. "He's kind of a wreck."

Xander leaned up to look at the person who was speaking.

"Huh?" He gasped when he saw her. This was most definitely not a girl.

The unicorn in front of him was purple. Her hide was as dry and flaky. It was even cracked in a place or two. But she was much cleaner than Ronk. And her eyes seemed to line up just fine.

But this wasn't a normal unicorn, if such a thing even existed. She had the same eerie glowing yellow eyes as Ronk. There were a few flies buzzing around her. And her hooves were a greenish color. They almost looked rotten. Xander was meeting not just one zombie unicorn, but two.

"Are you kiddin' me?" said a scratchy voice from the woods. "I walk away from you jokers for two minutes, and you're already talking to the locals?"

Xander got to his feet and strained to look into the shadowy woods.

"You guys are nuts," said the voice as a figure stepped into the light.

Correction: Xander was meeting *three* zombie unicorns. This one was a faded red color. His mane was purple and ratty. His body was covered in dry cracks. He had a little less dirt on him than Ronk, but a little more than the female unicorn. His eyes glowed yellow as well, and his face looked like he had spent a lifetime not taking any guff from anyone.

"What is happening?" Xander managed to say through a quiet voice.

"Kid," said the reddish unicorn. "You just made contact with the other side."

CHAPTER FIVE

After a few minutes, Xander agreed to sit down on one of the nearby boulders in the clearing. That was when he heard the loudest "RONK!" anyone had ever ronked.

Xander looked over at the green unicorn. Ronk was no longer eating weeds. No, his lean face was now pointed toward the sky. Ronk's mouth was open wide. But that wasn't the weird part. The weird part was that a rainbow—an actual full-fledged beam of

every color in
the spectrum—
was shooting out
of Ronk's mouth
and into the air.

"Aw, Ronk,"
said the reddish
unicorn. "Not
again!"

"Go easy on him,
Blep," said the purple
unicorn. "It's not like you weren't just doing
the same thing."

"Yeah," said the one apparently named
Blep. "Doesn't make it less gross."

The purple unicorn shook her head. Her
green mane shifted in the breeze. She looked
at Xander. "Anyway," she said. "I'm Cradie."

"Oh," said Xander. He wondered why these unicorns weren't in a state of shock right now. Their friend was barfing a rainbow. "Um, hi?"

"And you are?" asked Cradie.

"I'm Xander. Um, is your friend OK?"

"Kid, he's never been OK," said Blep.

"To be honest," said Cradie, "we're not sure why he's doing that. It's just something we do now."

"You . . . barf rainbows?" asked Xander.

"That's one way to put it," said Blep.

"It's part of the . . . the *sickness*," said Cradie. "Part of having the virus, I guess."

Xander looked at Cradie. His eyes went wider. Which is saying a lot, because his eyes had been wide ever since he met these zombie unicorns.

"Don't worry," said Blep. He was standing behind the boulders. He scraped one of his rotten brown hooves against the stone. He was apparently trying to remove some green growing thing on the bottom of his hoof. It wasn't coming off. "We're not contagious or anything."

Xander hoped the unicorn was telling the truth. "But you're sick?" he asked.

"Kind of," said Cradie. She was seated on the boulder across from Xander. Her front legs were tucked under her body. Xander was glad he couldn't see her hooves. They weren't pleasant to look at, to put it mildly. "The thing is, we were normal unicorns, but then we got a space virus, and we had to walk through the Banish Desert, which is not near as fun as the Danish Dessert—but that's another story entirely—and then we dropped through the Western Portal and ended up on this mountain and Ronk can't stop barfing rainbows and either can we, if I'm being honest, and—"

"Cradie," said Blep. It was a single word, but the way he said it made it sound like a complete sentence.

Cradie stopped and caught her breath. "Sorry," she said. "I've always been bad at stories. I get excited to tell the ending, and I keep talking, and if no one stops me I'll keep going until people either fall asleep or—"

"RONK!" said Ronk from across the clearing. He was done barfing rainbows.

"Thanks, Ronk," she said. Then she looked back at Xander. "Blep better tell it," she said.

Blep sighed and walked around the rock formation.

"OK, kid," said Blep. "Get comfy. Have I got a yarn for you."

CHAPTER SIX

Blep started his story:

It all started about a week ago. But it didn't happen here. Not on Earth, or whatever you call this place. No, this story took place on Pegasia. It's sort of a magical dimension. We got insect fairies, rock giants, soda streams—all sorts of cool junk.

So there we were. The four of us. The three of us here, and one other guy. Thing is, we had different names back then. I'll tell you 'em, but you're gonna have to promise not to laugh, OK?

Cradie, she used to go by her official unicorn title of Grape Sorbet. You would hardly recognize her back then. She was this real bright purple. Smelled about as sweet as a candy store. (You got candy stores in this dimension, right?)

Then you got Ronk. Now he was always a little . . . off . . . I guess you could say. But still, Ronk used to at least have a vocabulary longer than a name tag. Back then, he went by Tapioca Pudding. Guy was the cleanest unicorn

you ever saw. Now I know you ain't seen no unicorns before us. So just take my word for it. This scuzzy weirdo used to be the picture of cleanliness.

There was another guy in our crew back then. Stalor. When they were giving out names, he drew the long straw. If you can't tell by the way Cradie over there is sighing, guy was what they called a dreamboat.

Plus, he was sort of the leader of our group. I didn't ever think much of him. But I don't think much of most unicorns.

I'm the last of the four. Now, again, I don't wanna hear any snickering out of you on this. My name was Raspberry Jelly. All right, fine. You gotta laugh, get it outta your system now. I'll wait.

We good?

Can I finish the story now?

OK.

So the four of us are playing a game of hoofball in the Brown Sugar Fields, and like usual, Stalor's hogging the ball. Then I see this shadow cover the whole field. It was like something huge coming from the sky. I looked up just in time to leap outta the way. It was an asteroid.

The thing crashes down, but it misses all of us. We're all OK. I get up, and me and Stalor, we go and check it out. It looks like some kinda green gas is leaking out of it. I don't pay that any mind. (Kinda wish I had now . . .)

Pretty soon, all four of us are gathered around this thing like it's a campfire, and we're about to break out the s'mores. All the while, we're all breathing in this weird green gas.

I got sleepy next. We all did. So I can't really tell you what happened. All I know is, when I woke up, this is how I looked. All zombie-fied and whatnot. All of us looked like creeps, even Stalor. Although again, from the way Cradie's sighing over there, it didn't seem to affect his looks nearly as much as the rest of us.

After that, we go into town. The rest of the unicorns, they start to freak out. To make matters worse, all four of us got this new hunger, you know? We're starving. And everyone in Pegasia . . . Well, they smell really good.

Good enough to eat!

Ronk there—he was only saying "Ronk" by this point—Ronk, he goes and tries to take a bite outta old Miss Vanilla Bean.

She didn't take kindly to that. I can't say that I blame her.

Next thing you know, I'm trying to bite the tail off of Cotton Candy Surprise. Stalor's trying to chomp into Carmel Smoothie right in the rump roast. And innocent Cradie there, she's trying to eat the hooves off of Lemon Drop.

We just couldn't do nothing about it. All we wanted to do was eat our former friends.

So the town got together and had a big meeting. It took less than five minutes for them to come to a decision. They voted to banish us from Pegasia for good. We woulda put up more of a fight, but Ronk was trying to eat Mayor Blueberry Strudel at that particular moment. We figured they had a good point.

Next thing we know, we're ushered out to the desert. There's this magical portal waiting there for us. They shove us through. It closes behind us. Then we wake up here, early this morning. All of us besides Stalor, that is. I got no idea where that guy disappeared to.

We came up with new names for ourselves first thing. The old ones didn't seem to fit no more. Plus, when we start thinking about all that sweet smelling stuff . . . well, it gets us acting like maniacs. Crazy hungry maniacs.

Anyway, that's it. You're up to speed.

Ball is in your court now, kid.

CHAPTER SEVEN

"And you barf rainbows," Xander said. Despite how long the story had been, Blep had left that part out.

"You're really hung up on that, ain't ya?" Blep answered.

"Yes, we barf rainbows," said Cradie. "They just sort of shoot out of our mouths when we least expect it."

"RONK!"

As if on cue, Ronk let fly yet another bright stream of multi-colored light.

"We're going to have to do something about that," said Xander, watching Ronk.

"We?" asked Blep. "What, you're part of our merry troupe now?"

"Is . . . is that OK?" asked Xander. "You'll need some help getting used to our world. Somebody will have to show you around and teach you about our culture."

"And for that we're gonna rely on some human kid we don't even know," Blep said.

"Blep!" Cradie said. "Tone it down a bit."

"The kid can take it," said Blep. "When we were back on Pegasia, how many stories did we hear about humans? These *people* get word of us, and they'll try to capture us. They'll lock us away. They'll run experiments on us! You guys know how it'll go. Humans can't be trusted."

"But he's not a human," said Cradie.

"Um . . ." Xander was going to protest, but he thought better of it. Better to see where Cradie was going with this.

"He's a *kid*," she said. "Kids still believe in magic. They don't want to destroy it."

"That's right!" said Xander. He was a little too excited. But he couldn't help it. Before today, believing in magic had never been a good thing.

"RONK!" said Ronk. He seemed to be agreeing. He was flashing his weird grin at Xander again.

Xander wished he wasn't. Ronk was missing more teeth than he had.

"It's settled then," said Cradie.

Blep looked at her. Then he shrugged. It was clear to Xander at that moment that for all Blep's big talk, Cradie was the one truly in charge.

"You're one of us," Cradie said. "Aside from the whole not-being-a-unicorn thing and the not-being-a-zombie thing and the not-barfing-rainbows thing."

"But no adults," said Blep. He still had to get the last word in. (Or the last warning, at any rate.)

Xander smiled. It was a weak smile, but he meant it. "OK," he said.

An awkward silence followed. No one knew exactly where to go from there.

Then Blep said, "So you got anything to eat on this planet?"

CHAPTER EIGHT

"Hey, Mom!" Xander said as he rushed into the back door of his house.

Xander opened the fridge and pulled out a head of lettuce, a bag of baby carrots, and a plastic bin of spinach.

"Somebody's hungry," his mom said, looking over from the table. She had a stack of papers in front of her and was grading them. It seemed to Xander that ever since his mom took her geometry teacher job at the high school, all she did was sit at the table and grade papers. "Listen, I'm making spaghetti and breadsticks tonight for dinner, so don't fill up too much," she said.

"It's just vegetables," said Xander as he ran back out the back door.

"Can't argue with that," he heard his mom say behind him.

* * *

"Whatcha got?" said Blep as soon as Xander set foot into the woods behind his small backyard. The Rainbow-Barfing Unicorns had been waiting patiently just behind the tree line. There were several bushes there that hid them from the house. None of Xander's neighbors had houses that overlooked his backyard, either. It was a somewhat private place, which was one of the reasons Xander loved to explore it so much. But it had never contained any magic. Until today, that is.

"I got all sorts of good stuff," Xander said. "You can eat it all separately, or I can whip up a quick salad or—"

"Salad?" protested Blep. He sounded shocked. Appalled even. "You want to feed us salad? What do we look like . . . Rainbow-Barfing Bunnies?"

"Are those really a thing?" asked Xander. "What do you guys usually . . . I mean, I don't know what unicorns eat."

"We can eat salad," said Cradie. She stepped forward. "Don't mind Blep."

"What?" said Blep. He was even more surprised now. "You're agreeing with him?"

"A few greens won't hurt anyone," Cradie said. She looked over at Ronk for some support. The gray unicorn already had his face buried in the spinach container. Suddenly, he stopped eating. He jutted his head up. He opened his mouth.

"Or I could be completely wrong," Cradie said, almost to herself.

"RONK!"

A bright rainbow shot out of the tree line and straight at Xander's house. Xander let his own mouth fall open. The rainbow was blasting through the back kitchen window. It was heading right for the kitchen table. Right for his mom.

"Shut your mouth!" Xander said.

"You shut your—" Blep started to answer.

"He's talking to Ronk!" Cradie interrupted.

Xander put both hands over Ronk's

mouth. But the rainbow shot through the cracks between his fingers. It continued to shine directly into the kitchen window.

Xander peered over one of the bushes. He saw the kitchen door begin to swing outward. His mom stepped out onto the back steps. She looked over at the rainbow shooting into her kitchen window. She placed one hand above her eyes to shade them as she strained to look into the woods. It seemed to Xander that his mom was looking right at him. He quickly slumped to the ground behind the bush.

"Xander?" she called. "Xander are you seeing this?"

"RONK!" Ronk answered. Xander tried to cover the unicorn's mouth once again.

"Shh!" whispered Cradie. It was loud for a whisper.

Xander's mom took a step down the stairs. Then another. Then she began walking toward the tree line.

CHAPTER NINE

"No matter what happens," Xander said in a harsh whisper. "Nobody say anything."

"RONK?" asked Ronk.

"Not even that," Xander whispered.

"RONK," Ronk answered, nodding his head. Xander doubted Ronk understood a word he had said.

Xander's mom was halfway across the yard by now. "Xander?" she called.

"Stay down!" Xander whispered at the unicorns. Cradie and Blep knelt down behind one of the bushes. The last thing they wanted was to be discovered by an adult human.

Unfortunately, Ronk stayed put.

"Down!" Blep whispered. Blep swung his hoof out and kicked Ronk's front legs out from under him. Blep collapsed, but his hind end was still propped up in the air.

"RONK?" Ronk asked. He appeared more confused than normal. Blep then swept Ronk's back legs out from under him.

"RONK!" Ronk said, making a loud thumping sound against the ground.

At the noise, Xander's mom froze in her tracks. She looked over in the direction of Xander and his friends. She strained again to see them.

"Xander?" she called.

Suddenly Xander leaped out of the bushes and onto the grass of the backyard.

"Hi, Mom!" he exclaimed.

"Whoa!" his mom said in reply. She took a startled step back. "Don't do that!" she said.

"Sorry," Xander said. He was trying to appear calm and collected. He was doing a terrible job of it.

"What were you doing in there?" his mom asked.

"Just playing," said Xander.

"I thought you were having a snack?"

"Having a snack and playing," Xander said. He seemed even more suspicious now. His mom was picking up on it.

In the bushes, Cradie's head was resting on the ground. To keep out of sight, she was crouching as low as she could get. Near her face was the bag of baby carrots Xander had brought out for them. She sniffed the bag. She certainly was hungry. She stuck the end of her face into the bag and began to eat as quietly as she could.

"Do you see that rainbow?" Xander's mom asked. Xander looked over at the kitchen window. The rainbow was still lingering in the air. Its colors were fainter now, but it was still there.

"No," Xander said for some weird reason.

"It's right there," said his mom. "You're looking right at it."

Xander turned his head and looked back at his mom. "Sorry," he said. "Don't see it."

"**CRAYYYYDIEEEEEEEE,**" screamed a voice from the bushes. A new rainbow shot from the bushes right at Xander's face. Before he could do anything, Xander's head was lit up with the colors of the rainbow.

"Xander!" his mom yelled.

Xander decided to play it cool. "What?" he asked.

"You're standing in the middle of a rainbow!" she said.

"No I'm not," said Xander.

"What?" Xander's mom said, caught by surprise. "Of course you are. Can you not see this?"

"I have no idea what you're talking about," said Xander.

He took a step forward to allow the rainbow to continue past him. The light struck the side of the house.

"I'm gonna go get my camera," his mom said. She ran back into the house. Xander stayed in place for another few seconds. Then he bolted back to the bushes.

"What was that?" he yelled.

"Sorry," said Cradie. "That was me."

"Yeah," said Xander. "I figured. You yell 'Cradie' when you barf."

"That's how we got our Earth names," said Cradie. "You should hear Blep."

"Did your mom see us?" asked Blep.

"No, but she will," said Xander. "Get back up to the mountaintop. I'll meet you there in an hour."

The unicorns stood up. They galloped up

the mountainside, quickly disappearing into the thick forest. Once they were out of sight, Xander heard his mom open the back door of the house once again. He exhaled in relief. Now he just had to figure out a way to explain the large horselike teeth marks in the leftover carrots.

CHAPTER TEN

"Everyone comfy?" Xander asked in a low whisper.

"No," Blep answered. "Not in the least."

To Xander, Blep seemed like the kind of unicorn who would find any excuse to complain. But tonight, Blep had a point. At the moment, he, Cradie, and Ronk were all crammed into a small walk-in closet in Xander's basement.

They were lying on the cement floor, trying to get comfortable for the night. The floor's cold surface had been covered by a few of Xander and Reagan's old sleeping bags. A few ratty old pillows were scattered about here and there.

"Sorry about this," said Xander. "We'll have to find you guys a better place to sleep tomorrow night. We don't really have stables here in the suburbs."

"This is fine, Xander," said Cradie. "We're good."

"What the heck is this supposed to be?" Blep said.

Using his teeth, he raised the sleeping bag he was currently using as a blanket. On the bag were a few brightly colored ponies. Some had unicorn horns. Others did not.

"Oh, that used to belong to my sister," said Xander. "It's from that old cartoon, *One Trick Pony*."

"That's an offensive term right there," said Blep.

"Oh . . . ," said Xander. "Really?"

"Yes, really. How about I call you a skinny two-legs?" Blep said. "You like that?"

"No," said Xander. "But I've been called worse." Xander looked at the ground. He was thinking about school again. He was thinking about Kelly. Cradie seemed to be the only one who noticed.

"It's fine, Blep," said Cradie. She shot her faded reddish friend a stern look. He sighed and slumped his head down on the floor.

"What's a cartoon anyway?" Blep said to himself.

Ronk stretched and kicked Blep in the nose. But Blep didn't say anything. He just shut his eyes.

"So, if you could just keep quiet until morning," Xander was saying, "and maybe keep the rainbow barfing to a minimum?"

"No problem," said Cradie. She smiled. Unlike Ronk, she only had one crooked tooth. "No one has barfed a single rainbow since dinner."

"Well," said Xander. "That's something."

"Yeah," said Cradie. "I think it only happens after we eat."

"Hmph," Blep said to no one in particular.

"Good night," Xander said.

He shut the door to the closet. Then he tiptoed upstairs. In the living room, his parents were watching television.

Xander walked past them.

"Hey," said his mom. "You better get to bed."

"I'm on my way," Xander said. He wasn't particularly great at hiding his emotions. So when his mom turned to look at him, she could tell he was worried about something.

"Everything OK?" she asked. "Do you have to give a speech or something in front of class tomorrow? I know how nervous you get."

"No," Xander said. "Everything's fine."

"How'd your wizard costume go over?" asked his dad.

"It . . . went over," said Xander.

His dad was asking him more questions, but Xander was already in the process of jogging up the stairs toward his bedroom.

"Good night!" Xander yelled from the top of the stairs.

If his parents responded, he couldn't hear them. He was already in his room and planning his next course of action.

CHAPTER ELEVEN

As it turns out, you can search your entire life for magic, but that doesn't prepare you for the day you find it. Xander spent a good half of the night trying to figure out what to do with the unicorns in his basement. When morning came, he managed to sneak down to give them each a bowl of cereal. When all three began barfing rainbows as expected, Xander rushed upstairs and shut the basement door. If his dad had noticed the rainbow light shooting out the crack under the door, he hadn't mentioned it.

At school, Xander found it impossible to concentrate on his studies. He was tired from getting barely any sleep. And even though his mind kept racing, he kept dozing off. At one point, when he fell asleep during the history lesson, the teacher called on him. Xander's head shot up from its position in the crack of his textbook.

"Rainbows!" he shouted.

The class laughed. Xander's face turned beet red. The teacher just sighed and called on someone else.

Xander couldn't see a solution to his problems. How does one go about hiding three Rainbow-Barfing Unicorns from the world? And where could he possibly keep them? What could he feed them that wouldn't result in rainbows shooting out of every window in the house? He was so overwhelmed, he barely felt the tap on his shoulder as he waited in the lunch line.

"Hey," said Kelly. She had been standing behind him for the better part of three minutes, and Xander hadn't even noticed her. That was probably a world record. "You OK?"

"Huh?" said Xander, snapping back to reality. "I'm fine. Thanks."

"You look awful," Kelly said.

Xander shrugged and then turned back around. This was the last conversation he needed right now.

"I don't mean that as jerky as it sounded," Kelly said.

"Uh-huh," said Xander.

"Hey," said Kelly. "See any gnomes on your way home from school yesterday?"

"No," said Xander. His voice was cold.

"Are you mad at me?" asked Kelly.

"No," said Xander in the exact same tone.

"You know I wasn't laughing at you yesterday," said Kelly. "You know that, right?"

Xander didn't answer.

"I smile when I'm feeling awkward," she said. "And Andy always makes me feel awkward. It's like his secret talent."

Xander still didn't say anything. He believed her, but that didn't mean he was ready to stop being mad at her.

"Well, I hope everything's OK with you,"

said Kelly. "At least you get to go home and have a fun weekend.

Xander remained quiet. Kelly was probably talking about working at her aunt's apple orchard again. She went there almost every weekend even though her aunt couldn't afford to pay her. Apparently, the orchard didn't make much money. It was built next to the city dump. The smell kept most people away.

"I get to go and listen to my little sister complain," said Kelly.

Xander looked back at her. She'd certainly gotten his interest. She wasn't talking about the orchard at all.

"She's having a birthday party," Kelly said. "And she's all upset because the pony ride guy canceled. That's all she wanted for her birthday. Now we're never going to hear the end of it."

Xander thought about the *One Trick Pony* sleeping bag downstairs in his house. Then he thought about the creatures probably lying on it at that exact moment.

"Anyway, if you're not too mad at me, I was hoping you would come and keep me company," said Kelly. "At the party, I mean. Mom said I could invite one friend. You know, so I won't be bored out of my mind."

Xander smiled. He didn't mean to. But Kelly had never invited him anywhere. Let alone as her only guest.

Before he could stop himself he said, "I know where we can get some ponies!" When he saw the smile on Kelly's face, he almost didn't mind blurting out that sentence.

CHAPTER TWELVE

"Guys, I need a favor," said Xander as he threw open the basement closet door. But there was no one there. The only thing he was greeted by was a terrible, terrible smell.

Xander learned two things in that moment. The first was that he was apparently talking to himself. The second was that Rainbow-Barfing Unicorns do not smell good when left in small areas.

"Guys?" he said as he looked around the rest of the basement. He checked behind the water heater. He looked in the storage area under the wooden staircase. "Guys?"

Xander walked upstairs. His mom wasn't home at the moment. She had left a note on the table saying she was out getting groceries. His dad wouldn't get home from work for two hours yet, and his sister was busy at soccer practice. If he was going to talk to the Rainbow-Barfing Unicorns, now was the ideal time.

"Guys?" Xander said again. There was no answer. He walked outside.

Maybe . . . *maybe* it had all been his imagination. Zombie unicorns? That couldn't be a real thing. Maybe it was just his mind helping him deal with a particularly bad day at school. Maybe he'd just made the whole thing up—

But he wouldn't need to complete that particular thought. Because that's when Xander heard a familiar sound coming from the side of the house.

"RONK!"

Xander turned the corner to where the thin alley of concrete stood between the side of his house and the brown picket fence that his father kept threatening to paint but never did. There were the three Rainbow-Barfing Unicorns near one upset green trash can.

Xander said, "What are you doing?"

But Xander knew exactly what they were doing. They had knocked over the large plastic trash bin and were busy chowing down on last week's garbage. Even Cradie, the most reasonable of the bunch, was currently eating a brown banana peel.

"I can get you some real food!" Xander said.

"No need," said Blep, busy chewing on a bag full of green grapes. They had actually started out as purple grapes. But now they had a nice fuzzy mold growing on them. "We're good," Blep said. Then he leaned his head up, opened his mouth and . . . just burped.

Xander was cringing, waiting for the newest rainbow to shoot through the sky. But none came.

"You . . .," he started to say before Cradie interrupted him.

"We're not barfing rainbows," she said.

"Turns out this stuff is easy on the old digestion," said Blep.

"But that's garbage," said Xander.

"One man's garbage is another unicorn's afternoon buffet," said Blep.

"That's not a real saying," said Cradie. She bit into an apple browner than even Ronk's teeth.

"Honestly?" said Blep. "This is probably number two on my personal list of satisfying foods. It's good stuff."

Cradie nodded in response.

Xander thought about it for a moment. If this was the second best food to Blep, what was the first? Then he remembered their time on Pegasia. And he remembered how they had tried to eat their sweet-scented friends. Xander wondered if he'd be tempted to take a bite out of a unicorn that smelled of pure butterscotch. He wasn't really sure.

"Well, I'm glad everyone is in a good mood," said Xander.

"I don't like where this is headed," said Blep, looking up from his meal.

"Sooo," said Xander. "How do you guys feel about kids?"

CHAPTER THIRTEEN

"I can't believe I let you talk me into this," said Blep. Xander hit him in the face again with the powder puff. "Argh!" Blep exclaimed.

"You've gotta keep it down," Xander said. Xander looked back over his shoulder in the direction of Kelly's yard. It was only a few blocks away from his own. "We can't let anyone know that you can talk."

"Yeah, Blep," Cradie whispered. "You're the one who's all freaked out about science labs and the human government and all those lame old unicorn tales."

"Every story's got some truth to it," Blep said. His eyes were shut tight. If he dared open them, he risked getting an eyeful of makeup foundation.

"RONK," said Ronk, nodding his head. He seemed to be agreeing. No one was sure who he was agreeing with.

"Then all the more reason to stay quiet," Cradie said.

Blep did as she asked. It was kind of hard not to, especially now. For the first time since they'd been infected with the zombie virus, Cradie looked like her old self. Through the use of his mom's makeup, baby powder, and an art set he had gotten for his birthday from his grandma, Xander had given Cradie a bright purple makeover.

Sure, you could tell she was wearing makeup. But there was no such thing as a purple pony anyway. With Xander's help, Cradie looked like a regular pony that had been decorated for a child's birthday party. Even her unicorn horn didn't look out of place. With a little luck, these disguises would work.

Ronk shook his mane. Baby powder flew all over the surrounding woods. More than a little got on Xander.

Xander had to admit it to himself. It was going to take a whole lot of luck.

After a few more puffs of homemade red foundation, Blep's makeup was finished.

"OK, guys," Xander said. "Here goes nothing."

Cradie picked up the reins that she and the others had agreed to wear. If they were going to pass as show ponies, then they needed to look the part. Xander reached over and took the leather strap from Cradie's mouth.

"Don't worry," Cradie said to Xander. "We got this."

"Just no talking, OK?" asked Xander.

"RONK!" Ronk yelled in response.

This was going to take all the luck in the universe.

CHAPTER FOURTEEN

"This is so amazing," Kelly said. She walked over to Xander and gave him a huge hug. Xander blushed. "Just look at them!" Kelly said. She pointed across her front yard to her little sister and her friends. "They're having the time of their lives."

"I'm glad," said Xander. In truth, he wasn't feeling glad at all. He wasn't feeling anything other than nervous.

"How did you get them to be those weird

colors?" asked Kelly. She was looking at the Rainbow-Barfing Unicorns now.

The three were walking around in a circle, each with a different child riding on his or her back. Blep, Cradie, and Ronk each still wore their reins. The reins were tied to a pole in the center of the yard. Like the paint, the ropes were all a part of the act. They needed to appear like real ponies to any suspicious eyes. One slip up and everything would come crashing down around them. Everything today had to go perfectly.

"What weird colors?" Xander said jokingly.

"I don't understand how you have ponies and I never knew about it," Kelly said. She was looking back at Xander now. She was smiling larger than normal.

"I'm full of secrets," Xander said. That might have been the first completely true thing he had said since they got there.

Kelly laughed.

"What time is it?" she asked all of the sudden. It was as if she had just remembered something extremely important.

"Four o'clock," an adult said, butting into their conversation. Xander didn't know the strange woman. She was dressed in jeans and a flannel shirt. Her gray hair was in a ponytail, a style that looked much too young for her. But she had a kind face and smiled at Xander after answering Kelly's question.

"Oh!" shouted Kelly. "Time for cake!"

Kelly ran inside in a hurry. Xander straightened his back. This entire party was going better than expected. He had set out wanting to make Kelly happy, and he thought he had done just that. Her sister was certainly having a good time. Better yet, not a single adult at the party suspected that the ponies entertaining their children were secretly Rainbow-Barfing Unicorns.

"Happy birthday to you!" Kelly sang as she stepped out of the house. The rest of the party instantly joined in. All but Blep, Cradie, and Ronk, of course. The three unicorns seemed confused by the tradition. But then they noticed the large sheet cake in Kelly's hands.

"Frosting," Blep whispered under his breath. His mouth fell open. He started to drool without even realizing it. "It smells like . . . like home."

"RONK!" Ronk shouted.

Xander's eyes went wide. "Oh no," he said under his breath.

Ronk reared up on his hind legs and then darted toward Kelly. The reins restraining the ponies easily pulled right off of the pole. Xander hadn't even bothered to tie the ropes tightly in the first place.

"No," Xander said, louder this time.

Despite knowing better, Cradie and Blep weren't having any luck restraining themselves. They were as bad as Ronk at the moment. All three unicorns were sprinting toward Kelly and her cake.

"No, no, no, no, no," Xander said. But he didn't move. He couldn't move. He was frozen in his tracks. He had no idea how to even begin to handle this.

Kelly opened her mouth to scream, but she didn't even have time. In an instant, she was lying on the ground. All around her were pieces of the smushed cake. On her belly stood Ronk, his face buried in a large piece of the chocolate goop. Blep and Cradie stood on either side of Kelly. They, too, had their faces smothered in the remains of the sheet cake.

Xander stayed frozen. His mind raced. Then Ronk raised his head. Xander knew what was coming. Ronk was about to barf a rainbow in front of the entire neighborhood.

CHAPTER FIFTEEN

Xander swallowed the lump in his throat. This was his only chance.

"If I could have your attention!" Xander yelled over the chaos of the party. Xander was louder than even he expected. Every eye in the party was focused on him. Even the Rainbow-Barfing Unicorns were looking up from their snack. Xander's palms began to sweat. This was something close to his worst nightmare. But he had no choice.

"Everyone I've ever met has told me that magic isn't real," Xander said. He was surprised. He sounded much more confident than he really was. "But now, for our grand finale, I'm about to prove you all wrong!"

Xander looked at Kelly. She was still lying on the ground. Xander managed a weak smile. Then he shouted, "If everyone would please direct your attention to the magical unicorn named Ronk!"

Looks of concern began to vanish from the faces of the party guests. Even the adults began to suspect that the ruined cake was all part of the show. From her position on the ground, Kelly wasn't so easily convinced.

"Behold!" Xander yelled, just as Ronk bellowed his own name. Perhaps the brightest rainbow ever barfed shot from Ronk's mouth and into the sky. A stunned hush took ahold of the party guests. Kids and adults alike stared in silence. Then suddenly, the woman in the flannel shirt and ponytail began to clap. A parent at the party joined in. Soon the entire crowd was clapping and cheering wildly.

They had never seen anything like the show in front of them. They were all sure it was a magic trick. They were certain that what they were marveling at was a simple illusion. But they were still amazed. This young man named Xander could certainly put on quite the performance.

Xander looked over at Kelly. She had managed to shove Ronk off of her and was getting to her feet. She dusted off what cake she could from her pants. As Cradie and Blep each began to barf a rainbow, Kelly caught Xander's glance. She shook her

head. And then she grinned. Before Xander could realize what was happening, Kelly was laughing right along with the rest of the party guests.

"This is the best birthday party I've been to," said the woman with gray hair and the flannel shirt. "You have some kinks to work out, but I think I could help you with that."

Xander looked at the woman with a curious expression. He didn't respond.

"Xander, did you meet my Aunt Melinda?" Kelly said as she walked over near him.

Still confused, Xander managed to say, "Um, not really."

"She lives just south of town," Kelly said. "She owns the Montgomery Apple Orchard and Farm."

"Oh, the one near the—" Xander began.

"Yep," said Melinda. "So I'm always looking for ways to drum up new business, if you catch my meaning."

Xander wasn't sure he caught much of anything.

"I think your act here has real potential," she said. "But I have a few ideas for you."

Xander looked at the unicorns. Cradie and Blep were fighting over the last bit of squished sheet cake, while Ronk was busy running into the same wall of the house over and over again. It must have been all that sugar. Xander looked back at Kelly's aunt Melinda. He was certainly open to suggestions.

CHAPTER SIXTEEN

When he woke up, Xander checked
under the bed as usual. There was nothing
out of the ordinary. He didn't expect there to
be. He walked past the closet in his bedroom
and past the wardrobe in the hallway. There
was no time to check for other dimensions or
witches. He had a pretty full schedule today.
That stuff could wait until he got home.

After a bowl of cereal and a quick change of clothes, Xander gave his dad a high five and ran out into the garage. Before the garage door was even halfway up, Xander had already sped outside on his bike. He'd forgotten to close the door behind him yet again. His dad or mom would certainly tell him about that tonight. But Xander's mind was on other things.

It took about thirty minutes for him to bike to the Henderson Landfill on a good day. And this particular Saturday was certainly a good day. It was bright and sunny with just a hint of a fall breeze.

When he arrived, he parked his bike outside the open front gate of the landfill. Then he took a small plastic container out of his pocket. Inside was a pair of nose plugs. He popped them in and then walked through the gate.

"Guys!" he called. He walked past the piles of old, ruined tires, and the stack of mattresses that he had attempted to climb at least a dozen times so far. "Cradie? Blep?" There was no answer. Now more concerned, he called, "Ronk?"

"RONK!" came a familiar bray from across the yard. Xander hurried toward it. He rounded a large hill made up mostly of black and white trash bags. There, feasting on a particular open bag of what looked liked used coffee grounds and an empty bag of microwave popcorn, were the Rainbow-Barfing Unicorns.

Xander looked them over quickly. They had managed to get their stage makeup on all by themselves. And they did a pretty good job of it, too. There was hardly a hint of zombie-ness about any of them.

Xander said, "Guys, we're going to be late!"

Cradie looked up. She chewed the last bit of the paper popcorn bag and let out a quiet burp. Still no rainbow. Garbage really was the magic formula when it came to zombie unicorns. "You heard the man," she said to her friends.

With that, all three unicorns began to gallop toward the back gate of the dump. Xander led the way, arriving at the gate first. It was unlocked, and Xander pushed against it with his back. It popped opened. The four ran through.

They ran past the row of Golden

Delicious apple trees that lined the far end of the orchard. They hurried past the small barn that had been converted to the Rainbow-Barfing Unicorns' new stable home. And they didn't even slow their pace when they passed the stand that sold apple donuts. The smell was enticing, and helped to cover up the stench of the landfill next door. Xander even took out his nose plugs in order to catch a whiff of the sweet pastries as he jogged by.

When they reached the main yard, Xander and the Rainbow-Barfing Unicorns stopped to catch their breath. They stood behind the large building that Melinda had converted into a stage over a month ago.

A moment later, Xander and his magical friends walked around the building and up a set of stairs. Now on the stage, they looked out at their audience.

The stands were packed as usual. Ever since Melinda had agreed to showcase Xander and his "ponies" at her orchard, attendance had skyrocketed. People forgot the fact that her property neighbored the city dump. The garbage smell was no longer an issue. People just wanted to see the show.

Xander looked out at the staring faces. He breathed deep. He'd done this so many times, he hardly felt nervous any longer.

"Ladies and gentlemen," he began.

The murmurs in the bleachers came to an abrupt halt. Everyone wanted to hear what he had to say.

"Allow me to introduce," Xander shouted, "the Rainbow-Barfing Unicorns!"

The audience came to see tricks. They came to indulge their imaginations and to be dazzled by illusions. They had no idea that what they were seeing was very, very real. As Cradie, Blep, and Ronk pranced out onto the stage, Xander looked over to the front row. There, as always, sat Kelly.

The crowd may not have believed in magic, but Xander did.

There was all sorts of magic in the world. The Rainbow-Barfing Unicorns were only a small part of it.

RONK!

Height: 3 feet, 6 inches

Horn Length: 5 inches

Weight (before barfing): 130 pounds

Weight (after barfing): 115 pounds

Color: Puke-Green

Barf Color: Full Spectrum

Ronk is stinky, slimy, and oh-so gross. His vocabulary is limited to saying his name in a donkeylike bray. Often humorous and dim-witted, Ronk also has moments of clarity in which he is surprisingly wise.

GLOSSARY

banish (BAN-ish)—to send someone away from a place and order them not to return

digestion (duh-JESS-chuhn)—breaking down food in the stomach and other organs

dimension (duh-MEN-shuhn)—a place in space and time

gnome (NOME)—dwarflike old men from folktales and fairytales

illusion (i-LOO-zhuhn)—something that appears to be real but is not

portal (POR-tuhl)—a door or passage to another place

prophet (PROF-it)—one who predicts future events

spectrum (SPEK-truhm)—the range of colors shown when light shines through water or a prism

BARF WORDS

blow chunks (BLOW CHUHNGKS)—to barf

heave (HEEV)—to barf

hork (HORK)—to barf

hurl (HURL)—to barf

puke (PEWK)—to barf

ralph (RALF)—to barf

regurgitate (ree-GUR-juh-tate)—to barf

retch (RECH)—to barf

spew (SPYU)—to barf

throw up (THROH UHP)—to barf

upchuck (UHP-chuhk)—to barf

vomit (VOM-it)—to barf

yak (YAK)—to barf

JOKES!!

What do you call a
Rainbow-Barfing Unicorn's dad?

Pop-corn!

What kind of bow is
easiest for a Rainbow-
Barfing unicorn to tie?

A rain-bow!

What do you call
a smart Rainbow-
Barfing Unicorn?

An A-corn.

What does a Rainbow-Barfing Unicorn eat for breakfast?

Lucky Charms.

What did the Rainbow-Barfing Unicorn say when it had a sore throat from puking all day?

I'm a little hoarse!

What type of Rainbow-Barfing unicorn can jump higher than a house?

All of them. Houses can't jump!

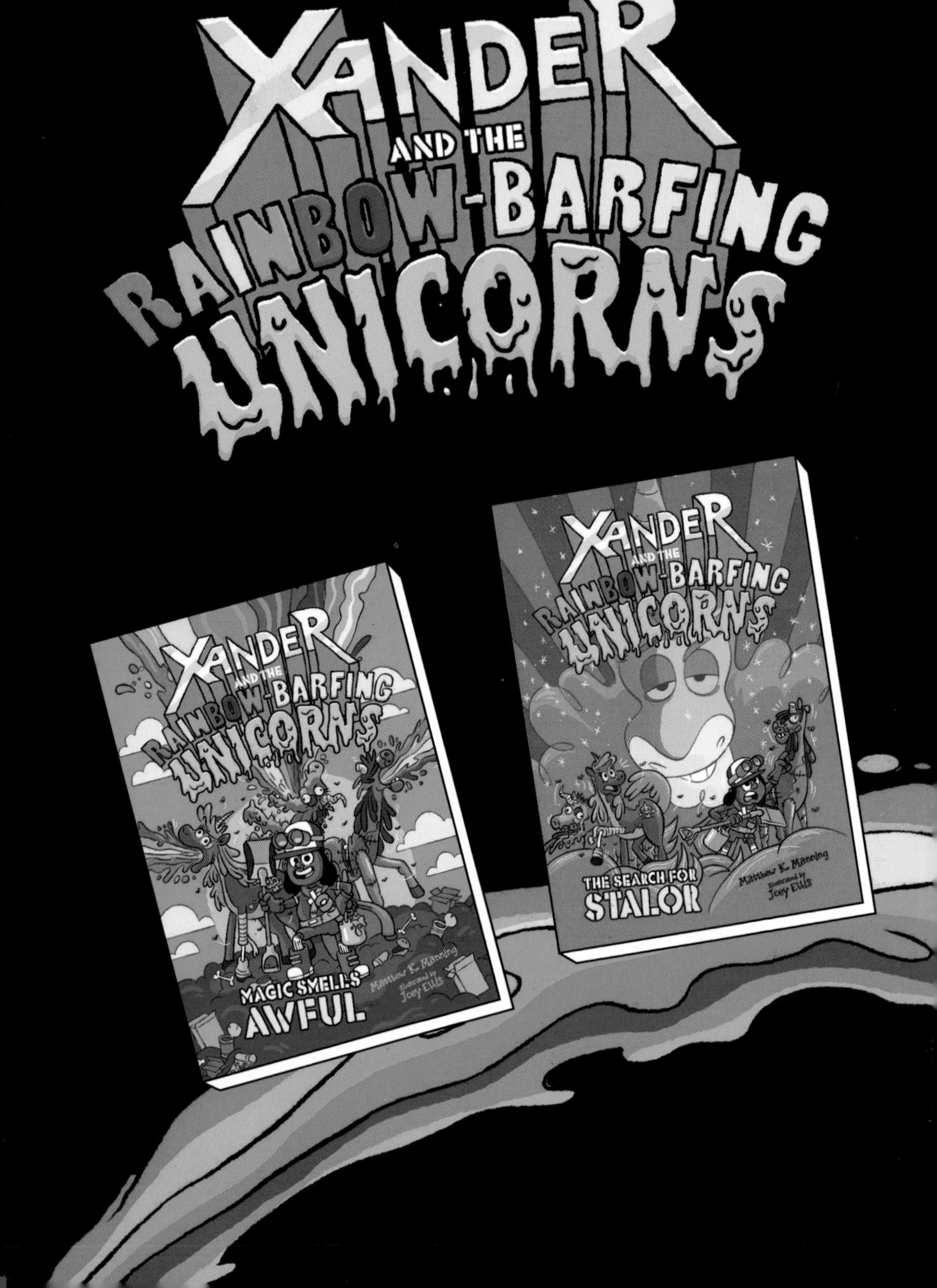
XANDER AND THE RAINBOW-BARFING UNICORNS
XANDER AND THE RAINBOW-BARFING UNICORNS
Matthew K. Manning
illustrated by Joey Ellis
MAGIC SMELLS AWFUL
XANDER AND THE RAINBOW-BARFING UNICORNS
Matthew K. Manning
illustrated by Joey Ellis
THE SEARCH FOR STALOR

READ THEM ALL!

AUTHOR

The author of over seventy-five books, Matthew K. Manning has written dozens of comic books as well, including the hit *Batman/Teenage Mutant Ninja Turtles Adventures* miniseries. Currently the writer of the new IDW comic book series *Rise of the Teenage Mutant Ninja Turtles*, Manning has also written comics starring Batman, Wonder Woman, Spider-Man, the Justice League, the Looney Tunes, and Scooby-Doo. He currently resides in Asheville, North Carolina with his wife, Dorothy, and their two daughters, Lillian and Gwendolyn.

ILLUSTRATOR

Joey Ellis lives and works in Charlotte, North Carolina, with his wife, Erin, and two sons. Joey writes and draws for books, magazines, comics, games, big companies, small companies, and everything else in between.